EPIPHANY

LOST IN THE TRANSLATION.

BY

JEITENDRA SHARMA

ISBN 978-93-5438-143-0
© Jeitendra sharma 2020

Published in India 2020 by Pencil

A brand of
One Point Six Technologies Pvt. Ltd.
123, Building J2, Shram Seva Premises,
Wadala Truck Terminal, Wadala (E)
Mumbai 400037, Maharashtra, INDIA
E connect@thepencilapp.com
W www.thepencilapp.com

Author biography

I am Jitendra kumar sharma(Jeitendra sharma), I don't call myself a poet, I love to write Lyrical poems, storytelling, and read whenver I can. from Philosophy, History, Mythology, and ofcourse the Mathematics. I never intended to write in a certain style but I love how each Poem can be written in a different style. Hope You would love to read it.

Writing is what I can do all day and night, it gives me a meaning in this meaningless life.

Contants

EPIPHANY

Author biography

Contants

Epigraph

Acknowledgements

Looped reality

Epiphany

mask

red flag

Dialectical materialism

metamorphosis

Arkham asylum

walk of pride

countryside

who am I

orchestra

fireball

autumn song

lettre à la lune

surrealism

atomo

Hikikomori

A forever

Non ducor duco

facet of time

apologies

see You

a million times

limitlessness

melancholy

Hippocratic oath

self heist

free world

fort without walls

shades of man

Kafkaesque

Epigraph

From french Revolution to the recent events in the Indian soil, I am facinated with the emotions which drive a man, to lose everything for a cause and purpose. I believe that Bhagat singh's dream was a total opposite of what we have today. This capitalist Society is creating spectacles which is far from reality, my poems are from every walk of life but in this book You will find a certain feeling of emancipation and relief from heavy pain of modern life.

Hope You will find a purpose in this, and spread the Revolution of this kind.

Thank You.

Acknowledgements

o all who had fall so that I could read them... to all writers and
ᵒoets, philosophers who

Looped reality

a mysterious child
it's cold out here
who could have abandoned it?
Hello! whose child is it?
no answers from shadowless streets
what should I do?
a remote area, danger animals out there
the child sleeping peacefully
as the world hasn't been doomed yet,
a beggar on the street
looking here and there
maybe searching for something
hey! mister, did you see my child?
I couldn't remember, where did I put it?
"surprised"
what? is it your child?
I don't believe it, You are the father?
what misery lies ahead for this little soul?
wait? I was also an orphan?
somebody dumped me too
is this the way history repeats itself?
what should I do now?
should I return the child to his father?
or, should I become his Godfather?
I haven't seen any child around here
You should search nearby
maybe You will find it?
"Beggar intoxicated with chemicals"
Oh! I will search for it in the morning

it's too late now
I should get sleep
and he walked away,
man came inside
couldn't resist looking at child
blood in his body became cold
the breath has stopped
as it was he! himself
what? how is it possible?
how, I am holding myself?
no this is nonsense!
I should leave this child outside only
this is something horrible
I will lose my mind?
and then he dumped him outside
this is how he remained orphan
a loop that will play again,

Epiphany

no discrete points
life switches, continuously
between birth and death
no defined path or there are infinite of them
the light turned into darkness
with no specific point to find out
the subtlety in mediocre minds
a process of isolation or
crowds that hide the emptiness
a smile that shields unwanted attention
or a desperate attempt to find someone
there is no ultimate truth
life itself comes with a paradox
live to die or die to live
liberated to accept restrictions
or restricted to be liberated
working classes live in a dilemma
revolution or a piece of bread
selfish creatures, the occupant of high classes
vomit milk to feed starved
a system that fails every time
hear the voices in the head
all those who couldn't survive one more day
an epiphany that leads to nihilism
binary thinking of good & bad
fighting for truth and lie
I saw a man smiling on the streets
He whispered " You are alone"
it's all inside Your head

nothing is real
it's an ultimate revelation
it's You all over
either love or hate
nothing is real
die or live
nothing matters;

mask

not to hide,
liberty to become what I am
a mask of imperfections
burn morality to the ground
unleash the hidden creature
bear the weight of it
as the grasses beneath mountains
feel the power of it
like a mighty sword in the hands of Lords
to bring justice to oneself
no more hiding the urges
to cover the weakness
that has existed in minds,
a birth to send shock waves across
the reaction of your upside-down cross
what you had done in closed rooms?
feel the taste of Your own medicine
the power to crush your foundations
a change in the equation
the new ruler is here
burn the houses on fire
let the peace die one more time
one more inequality
to justify all
few more blood drops on the streets
with no hidden lies
it will cut with a knife of truth
the causality is here
face the injustice of your past

sweat and blood
with iron rod
and no more hunger strikes
feel the agony of this mask;

red flag

fire!
the crowd couldn't disperse
rainwater mixed with blood
the streets are rivers of sacrifice
flowing in that river
I found the reasons
to raise voices?
to get bullets on the bare chest
I see!
the reasons
the bullets showering on crowds
food might not be cheaper than it?
Just a bullet in the head
no more demands for food
equal rights,
or questions to the authority
powerful hands
brutally crushing the hands behind the development
broken glasses on the streets
and a great walk
each scar will be noted down in history
the voice that has suffered
a silence will emerge
powerful than the voice
You strangle
today,
red flags were white
a symbol of peace
but,

You
the selfish creatures
the filthy worms of nature
who had left a few drops
after sucking most of it
came out of flesh
and colored the white
a resistance
that was born,
hang us
but remember
tomorrow
will be ours,

Dialectical materialism

a class struggle
shaping the future's struggles
a fight between manpower and machines
who'd not demand a life
out of a cycle that ruins the dreams,
separate institutions
timid characters are forced to born
a distinction, fuels the brands
who'd not like to wear those expensive Jeans
the symbols born out of imagination
have a price tag on them
however, a few could afford them
exchange values will put you on shame
the village would've survived a month on them
the surplus had given births to all slaves,
a class distinction
don't Judge them with name
names they can't afford
but are the reasons behind them
buy cheap and sell expensive
a common capitalist trend
to curb inflation
You don't let them born
all sweat and blood
goes into survival
how'd one come out of it,
cities are built on their ruins
all doors are closed
no dust from the village could travel to it

there is a lot hidden in names
once a while a traveller finds a way
to get arrested into the isolation of them
a depression caused by alienation
no worth of an individual
here,
everything runs by groups of slaves
no face, no identity of their own
just a price tag that is their worth,
thrown like a bag of garbage
when asked the question of existence?

metamorphosis

a metamorphosis, chaos into order
an illusion seems so stable
the advent of madness in the milieu
projection of individualism into the crowd,
a single match stick that initiates a fire
burning down the whole empire
a man hiding horrors within himself
a chance to fire guns without being responsible?
who'd not want to kill?
an inner desire to see others suffer
screams that would become melody to the ear
enough of hiding, beast craving inside
all are bloodthirsty like a vampire in the night
revenge, we want it from the bottom of our heart
a chance to crush the opposition
that won't let us feed our dogs
see the nightmares that reflect our reality
don't fear it, go nearby and have a talk
touch the ugliest looking creature with lust
see the metamorphosis
You are one of it
the trickery of brain would no longer play the game
end of symmetry I've broken the chain
now look into the mirror
don't feel ashamed
we all are our nightmares
who want to escape the reality
surrounding ourselves with beauty
there is a collective brainchild of us

weak, deprived in exile
we've abandoned him starving
collecting garbages near downtown
outskirts of our great cities
there lives a bane
who would survive
and come back to haunt us
there will be questions?
and the destructions of our dreams
end of fool's paradise;

Arkham asylum

spiralling down into the abyss
betrayal of entrusted one's
selfish creatures standing all above
I see their smiles
and hear their laughs
from the corners of a hidden place
behind them, in disguise
I see the true nature of the mask
the delusion that I've created
applauds that I hear
all love
and the talks in my head
You are not real
Just a reflection of my needs
acceptance is what one seeks?
the turmoil that hides me
all one asks is a material need
nobody likes an ugliness
no depths are greater than despair
uncertainty catches the fire
a limited source of happiness for both
stop! drawing more
or should I quit the desire
too much in my thoughts
I see the espionage
the conspiracies that are being made
I am standing behind your back
looking it into great details
after all, it is all inside my head

I see the world as I want
and creates things that could torture me
to feel the agony
that make things real
however, I know the delusion
of Arkham Asylum!

walk of pride

Me, and You
walking together again
years have passed
still, I remember the old times
little feet of mine
and giant shoulder of Yours
holding the weight of future
I never heard You complaining
about life
how ungrateful it has been, indeed?
the struggles You have been through
the hardship of old times
a self-made success
with compassion for others
helping hands of Yours,
How ungrateful I am?
I never wanted to be like You
afraid of all this suffering that honesty brings
but I regret it, as I couldn't be like You
I lack courage and don't have that mighty heart as yours
I see the strength in Your ideas
the conviction to overcome all problems,
walking again with You
reminds me of old times
things I couldn't tell You
but I know You are the 'Man'
growing-up with values You have taught
I know the values of human life
the equality and Justice

for which one has to fight
thank You
for
walking beside me,

countryside

distant trees and clouds
a silence worth of million words
I see the moving frame
the still painting of nature itself
mud-houses welcoming at the door
first asked to have some water
before enquiring about whereabouts
the lost culture of ours
value for human, not the possession,
leaves are storyteller here
falling, floating, in air
wild animals are not caged here
each footprint tells us a story
someone couldn't afford a pair of shoes again!
a smile that hides the secret of lives
old shivering hands touching me with compassion
excited to hear the story of my world
what should I tell them?
time is much slower here
no one is running here and there
no medical shops around
I see a few old men laughing aloud
the sun is hiding behind the beautiful scene
a warm glass of milk with a piece of Jaggery
no running heartbeats about sharemarkets
a steadiness lies within them,
the smell of that coal smoke
a small room hiding a long history
I see them happy together

the old man and his wife
a life with no anxiety and disorder
no rush in the blood
nothing last forever
but that smile would, inside me
the way it touched me
'a countryside'
I wish I could go back in time
and stop those fools
who have abandoned the heavens
in search of more
I would've been happy with less
at least, I had people around to share with me
share their pain and happiness
running barefoot, without hesitation;

who am I

walking, running, hiding
ln search of a shelter
who am I?
a crisis within me!
not fond of Your theories
I will search mine
not mining the earth
I will dig a hole into the sky,

look around me
there are stars within
bursting out in desire
but calm like moon
I see the real meanings
a system
that exploit
a man
who kills others
a child
who is under the bed
fear running in veins
People are shouting outside the door,
peace will not come
lust is more powerful
people aren't good anymore
all are searching for someone to blame
then hang him in cold-blood
with all heads down
slaves can't rise above hate

don't touch me with Your blood-stained hands
I' am not one of You
Yes! I'm Insane
Lost sanity long ago
a fight for Justice is the aim;

orchestra

(music in the background)
a personal orchestra
I hear the sound of rolling tears
a girl
a smile!
and a lot of memories,
a storm had hit
without warning
leaving scars on her
like a claw of wolf had struck her
and she learned the art of silence
not to disturb motion-less particles,

sleeping to hide the wet pearls
dreams have fallen into whirls
no more peaceful nights
meaninglessness
following each step
no more stairs to count on
lies are far from reality,

a curse that has travelled miles
following the man
no one skips the fruit of sin
a ghost that follows us all
counting stars at night
riding rainbow in daylight
sliding in circles
reaching to destination

it hunts the smile
the inner storms invite it
to come and play with our minds
and we fall into our reality,

life comes in moments
that small-detailed tik of clock
flowing like wind
circling the dreams
in the night when the city sleeps
she is awake
counting the tik
breathing to survive
but in hope
that world would end
no tomorrow
nothing more to borrow,

she is young
in her late teen
learning a few things
look at her
a pale dark skin
drained of blood
grasping world of other's desire
and the orchestra stops!
a life has ended in this game of fire;

fireball

red
fireball
on the sky
rising above the horizon,

a start, from the end
a cycle
to roam around,
walking day & night
still,
not exhausted
sailing through the sea of darkness
reaching the zenith
to fall free from above
and rise again
to make the world live more,

a promise of all mothers
to have bread & milk
tomorrow,
responsibilities of angels
to feed them in dreams
night has to die, again
the sun has to rise
again,

autumn song

eyes!
falling into it
flowing beneath your hairs
the warmth of breath
don't close Your eyes
let me sail in and out
all the tears
which is inside, will come out now
the moments like this
holding Your hands
and singing songs of autumn
we could fly away
into the distant stars
with the wings of our dreams
look at the moon
smiling the light away,
hope!
we would meet again
with the drops of rain
and the wind that freezes our heart
beneath those trees
we'd fall again
and get drunk in the passion
waiting to touch those lips
into a deep state of sleep
peace of hearts!
and those silly drops rolling down to the cheek;

lettre à la lune

walking
with someone
I had little acquaintance,
on the stairsteps
bragging
about the stars
opened up like a fresh soda Can
with sparkles of nervousness
I bumped into the little known world of words
a beauty that I had ignored in past
lost inside mind
the hidden secret of imagination
found the desire to explore
to say it aloud
a redemption or an expectation
whatever, but the light weightiness
the erstwhile me never had such feelings
l found refuge after a within-exile
like soul had come back
with a touch of emotions
a state of numbness was over
I could now hear the music again
the magical instruments within my heart
a sharp u-turn inwards
I found the meaning of life
a smile
cost me all my sin
a new birth
born out of ashes of past

sometimes innocence could bring a change
and,
a smile with a heavy heart
could bring dark clouds over you
the wrath of nature
feel the salty rains of the pain
look at her
and those eyes
God must be wondering
an unexpected turn
let them burn
in the fire of separation
I see the moon, so do You
let the moon read my letter to You
whispering to You
let him tell
all the desires I have
my restlessness, sleepless nights
the emptiness of my place
and the echoes of your voice
hitting the wall of hopes
weaving the dreams
that one day
we'll see the moon together
holding hands
lying down
without saying anything
we will talk together again;

surrealism

corrupt minds, fear-mongers
fat belly digesting moral values
hunger has chosen the side
starving bones turning into products
walking miles to sweat the blood
a smile that can not afford expenses
medical bills and costly injections
who'd buy the pen, when survival is at stake?

selfish brazen society laughs at them
washing bloodstains from the hands
we produce more than one could consume
I don't see Gods visiting those slums
on the outskirts of the beautiful heaven
a mirror that reflects the poverty
installed in the outlets with a smile
I don't like the tomatoes let's put it out
they can't see, standing outside of the window
picking the leftovers from the dustbins
nowadays I use sanitizer for hygiene!
it cost me three hours of hard labour
to put things out of my hands
but it seems as they are immune to it
sitting in the corner, I ordered
two days worth of hard labor
and the funny thing
I left the tomatoes
which millions can't afford!

atomo

the scattered grain of sands
floating above the sea
with the blow of wind
reaching new heights
wings of uncertainty, high hopes
eyes at heaven, trying to touch it
individual particles fighting with each other
in a meaningless race
all will settle down at last
wild-wind will take rest at night
the cold-water will not welcome grains
the wetness will sink it low
game of destiny, indeed!
someone will walk over it
crushing it further-down
all hopes have sunk with the sun
moon has gone extinct
the heaviness of the heart
the unwanted situation at the door
knocking it down,

a brighter moon
with all new hopes
distance is less now
the sea could feel the weight of it
trembling earth
there is life beneath the sea
one more chance, a tsunami
to rise with all weight

to the zenith of surface
a quantum dance of earth at its axis
the force of nature at the service
a fair game of hide-and-seek
to hide the selfness
and to seek the union with the world
to attain a state of freedom
freedom from all sin, and the existence
to become shining sun at night
and the full moon in the daylight,

Hikikomori

a treehouse
far into the wild
no metal sounds
Just water drops falling from leaves
group of birds humming songs
sunshine at Your face
a moon shining in the shadow
a morning in the heaven
no gods! Just Me and You
I could hear the beats
calling for me
even in dreams
the sweet moan of You
breaking the silence of eternity
a night in Your arms
burned into ashes now
boundaries between us
no one is here to teach us
the morality of an immoral world
a life that has escaped the reality
into the illusion which is more than real
I see the depths of our hearts
all world could fit into
but we couldn't fit in that world
dead fish flowing with the flow
reached into the sea
a few tried to climb the stairs of water
survived the claw of dark society

running inside the wildness
eating apples from the tree of love;

A forever

a forever
eternal or timelessness
a momentary eye contact
seems lasting forever
a few words
resounding forever in head
a glimpse of a smile
playing in the loop forever
that beautiful red flower
dying between pages of the book, forever
an emotion inside the heart
hiding from the world, forever
a rage that could burn it all
sparking through eyes, forever
a hope to see moon together
living inside with each breathes, forever
to die somewhere near
so that one could visit, forever
to build a small house inside a forest
to escape from reality, forever
using words to describe all this
so that it could live, forever
shutting doors from inside
waiting for someone to come
a forever
how long is it?
for some

a moment
and for others it is timelessness,

Non ducor duco

creation, a miracle
birth of a creature
a Goddess who bleeds
lives above the thorns
with a magical spell from the fairytale
creates another who breathes
not the God who destroys
but a Goddess who sacrifices
feed her blood to a monster, or, a victim
unbearable pain, hundreds of breaking bones
source of this world, verticle orientated ellipse
patriarchal legends of Gods
de-jure of this system
like the statue of liberty, the Motherland Calls
a symbol of greatness, equality, and power
a creator who pays the price
"Non ducor duco"
a command to walk behind
born to trace the path laid down by gods
not to cross the lines drawn by a master
a slave who has the power of creation
without which the life would seize to exist
fierce worrier of the battle
forced to be caged, inside big wall
tethered with the old rituals and tradition
curtailing equal probabilities of success and opportunities
curbing the growth towards liberation
stop this hypocrisy, where is the democracy?
no equality to raise voice

a goddess, is chained, is a creator
an imposter sitting on the throne
dictating lies and fraud
egalitarian minds are numb
no one sees the real goddess, the creator of all;

facet of time

tranquillity in the eyes
I have forbidden the fragile thoughts
none shall interfere with
the business of the wise mind
depths of the cosmos
lights that carry the world with it
yet, weightless and superfast
the burden of the world made it stop
the time is sitting along, having a chat
about the lives which run according to it
birth, death, and all other drama
like a perfect stage of a storyteller
with the swing of the hand
the music floating in the mind
I hear the pain of the empty sits
as no one is here
to see the loneliness of the man
inside the womb of the creator
a serpent coiled with sin
looking at the possible pathways
waiting for pray to come
to attack with the reality
the reality of mortality, of a man
who live a life in dreamland
far in the woods
beneath the mighty sun
seek pleasure at nights
praising the silvery light of the moon
see me not

thus, the sun speaks out!
a blind man
couldn't be blinded again
thus seek within
with those eyes that see without light,

like a bird that dies without flying
a fish without swimming
so the man dies
without looking inside
with the darkness of his deeds
create the hell which burns without fire
and rain that melts the very skin
run into despair
not to put faith in those idiots
who couldn't see without light
a blind man thus lead the all, who have closed the eyes
I am the wisdom
first, you need to fall
into the darkness of your soul
thus comes the saviour of all
a man, who doesn't seek
an ant, who doesn't eat
a wolf, who doesn't howl
a moon, who doesn't shine
one, who forgets who is he?
live the life
without burden
and feel no pain
and share no time with time
as it crosses the illusion created in time;

apologies

I've come so far
across the bridge
built on the faith and reverence
time had been long since its inception
so the walk of mine
no direct path as no one had walked before
no traces except the ashes of those
who burnt their lights creating it
the footsteps are not clear
one can see the stubble grasses
there are fewer probabilities to find the right one
I seemed to enjoy the wrong ones
the curiosity that stars brings
and the red colour of dawn
fascinating creatures crawling inside
see the past in those old eyes
an expectation!
a hope on which one thrives
see the wrinkles
on the hands
which were the might once
working hard to procure more
to feed the empty stomach of all
walking miles in the wild
scared, not at all
one who faces the hunger, fear no more
but there is fear inside
as the building is standing on faith
brick by brick

sweat and blood
how could one waste it anymore?
apologies!
but one should do more
to feel those empty stomach
so that all could sleep
to wake-up again
in the world of hope
to see impossible dreams
with the rise of one more sun;

see You

I see You
rolling in my head
picture of You
a moment that caught me
looking at You
I felt the emptiness of the world
poise, sacrosanct breath
the silence between Your voice
a goddess!
disturbing the tranquillity of life
a calm wave, suddenly rising above
floating above the surface, a walk of Yours
feather falling from above
and I am waiting down
looking above to hold You
between my arms, a daydream of mine
a barrier of anonymity couldn't stop desires of mine
a hope to touch the feather in my hand
to feel the beauty of Yours
I know the limit of our feets
but the heart won't stop
it would travel miles to wake you up
with the sweet voice in Your ear
a whisper! a breath that is familiar
a dream, but real
a goddess, but in human form
I would wait millions a time
to see You again
and wait

before dying
to hear whispers of You
in the end
I would be with You;

a million times

millions!
millions of miles away,
stars! died millions of time
still looking bright
millions of miles away
I see the vast night sky
millions of clustered suns
Hope! of millions
promise to come back again
One day in millions of years
it would die
a death, that would take millions of years
shifting of spectrum
Millions of them, like me
or like You
a million-time meeting You
living with Hope
that in a million time, we'd meet once again
to see the birth of a million stars again
or, to die with one in a million
I see the vast night sky
and a million dream
that die each night
and born again with the dawn
dies at a million
and born with one
the closeness that brings warmth
belittle the millions who are at a distance
like the one flower in white snow

red as the blood of youth
and young as the virgin desire
like sands at the beach
millions together
like the herd of sheeps
that scatter when trouble comes
nothing stays forever
not even the millions
but one soul
that lives within
and another that finds One in millions;

limitlessness

Illusion or reality, self-contradictory
I see what exist
or I create reality
could a mind creates unseen
to perceive unreal
a mental condition, people say it
maybe a different reality
the illusion to Rest, but real to One
let's dive into crisis
to figure out the secrets
Certain questions, of all generations
enlightened ones
or illusionary in disguise
believe and faith
the ultimate tool to curb criticalness
in this vast spread space
and the ultimate knowledge of tinyness
I see the inevitability of an end
and a beginning,
was it a point of starting?
or continuation of wild energies
no end and no start
like an unremembered dream
all the agonies and melancholy
reminds us of our physical nature
and the hunger that blinds us
the impulsiveness of the animal inside us
reminds us of the beginning
but where to end?

evolution, will it end?
could one reach the perfection
the existence will seize
as one would know the emptiness, meaninglessness of life
not to fight with others
I see the enemy inside
the ignorance of the human mind
to accept the limit,
truth is limitless
and so the lives,

melancholy

a world to me
shadows of dark
see me now
scattered, flowing into pieces
miles between us
even thoughts couldn't reach You
a new world around me
teaching me to live without You
snakes bitting me to suck the venom out of me
venom, the world had put inside me
continuous sacrifices that one had to make
walking on the curses laid down for me
I touched the holy grail in You
enshrined within the shape of the heart
detested the separation that brought upon
expelled from the kingdom of heaven
a Goddess, sitting on the throne of the heart
pulled out of me, still beating in red
lost everything one could wish to have in a lifetime
fear to lose You, prevailing crisis midst of ultimate love
the head that holds itself high, bend in front of the stones
the rain was the envy of the tears of mine
as it had a greater purpose to drench itself
You had gone till the time sun had arrived
using the dark narrow paths that lead towards my sin
an untold bizarre part of the protagonist
a story devil whispered in the ears of antagonist
did You see the face that dares to speak out the truth?
felt the nerves of that cold past that hide behind that smile

don't try to find but still, eyes search for the face of Yours
wish that I would never have to face that innocent Face again
death would be better than answering to puzzled eyes
hold me close now, as I am about to vanish
into those fairytales of Yours
You would find me within, whenever someone will touch You
and die each time a cold death in those warm moments;

Hippocratic oath

cold-blooded animals!
walking dead, no emotions
a beast disguised as a man
a plot to kill the last hope
black-heart darker than the night!
hell-bounded man, but where is the lord?
lord who took an oath to protect us
protect from the beast inside us
he must have heard the screams!
or the plot in the rotten mind
he must have not complied with it
Is he dead? or, coward
it is lame to blame karma, I see none!
stars, why couldn't You fall?
moon, how could You not move to help?
wind, You should have come to protect
fire, You must have had cried?
I see no reason, One must not go through this
either the heaven is full or the hell is empty
all good men are in heavens
and all cold-blooded animals are walking on the streets
How I would praise You, Lord, again?
Your children don't deserve such pain
thus, come and take the bow in Your hands
a fight is at the doors, please, hide no more!
thousands of Years have passed
nothing has changed, same agony different names
or You are just like one of us
who don't even dare in their dreams

who keep quiet at the moment of crisis
and then whisper the name
there is everything at the stake
come and, remember Your Hippocratic oath?
bring the Justice to all
don't wait for one to fall
come and rescue before the devil hits
all hands that praise You, could point at You?

self heist

self heist
losing ourselves on the outskirt
a drawn boundary serves well
to keep the secret inside
where one could look at the pit
without acknowledging reciprocation
we shut the doors, and leave ourselves out
with the coldblooded soul
who knows the deepest depths of our reality
and we refuse to hear the voices
an illusion to survive without trouble
the ignorant mind lives more
so the slave who can't bear hunger
as no standoff takes place in such a situation
We hide and run from ourselves
live with the poison that numb the rebel voices
I see the scared kid inside
craving for love and care
afraid to ask it loud
it creates the wall of self-hatred
and then the iceberg melts
with the touch of the right companion
one dares to pull out everything
that have been inside since inception
pour out the secrets
surrender the soul in front of the slayer
and bend down on knees
ready to accept the verdict
like a man ready to die in the Warfield

acceptance means a new life here
on the ruins of ourselves
we break the wall with permission
and dare to look into eyes
to see the forgiveness
which we couldn't bring ourselves
and it gives the relief, emancipation
a flower that would blossom again
with the warmth of some prophet
or goddess, who melted the coldness
with the power of innocence
hatred has gone
so the beast who eats itself
replaced with a competent heart
love could do wonders
either it could destroy the troy
or could save the Cleopatra;

free world

I could Just cut and lose
strings attached
pulling my flesh without mercy
so, I could run in the vast free lands
swim in the cold water of white ice
roar with the lions in their natural habitat
where I could speak with birds
or hear their masterpiece
an orchestra that sings the song of nature
no greed lies in here
in the depth of green grasses
I have seen the ants walking tirelessly
a sense of responsibility at the door
take me that land of peace
where I would wake up without worry
with no formalities of smile and happiness
and I could shed tears with wolves, staring at the moon
where no one will find the trace of the human race
no gunfights, no borders, no violence
Just survival instinct, and hunger that drives the killing
I would pray from falling stars
to turn me into a Jungle leaf
so, I could roam around with the wind
swim in the freshwater with fishes
or, become a firefly
so the stars would envy me
and I would tell everyone that I belong to stars
I had fallen in the past, but one day I will fly away
reach the zenith, kingdom of heaven

rule all the stars and command them to shine more
or fight a battle with moon
and tear it in parts
take me there in the land of absolute truth
where no lies reside
a place where hell means human kingdom
where I could see all colours except the red blood
and die in peace;
with a decaying body that would serve the next,

fort without walls

I was there
standing near shores
when troy was falling
I could feel the sense of embarrassment
the folk legend had come to an end
walls, which were standing for millennia, were falling
lords were shouting the folk phrases
a formidable man was breathing last breath
asked no help from anyone
fought with bravery and self-worth
hundreds of Achilles, fighting one
thousands of arrows, falling at him
standing on feet barely moving
the fort was inevitable to fall,
thus comes a prophet
preaching peace amid a bloody war
like sun throwing life everywhere
prophet of human minds, a philosopher
who could make the pain bearable
or, could find the meaning in a meaningless world
alone in front of thousands
without swords or arrows
cutting the darkness of the fort, we build around us
and lament its fall
an empire we rule within ourselves
with the unknown enemies;

shades of man

monsoon had come
sprinkling hopes in the eyes
a trapped feeling wanted to go
one wants to shout out loud
the pain that was kept in the past
buried under the ice of ages
a familiarity in unfamiliar face
came out of the closet of the dead,

ice had seized the warmth
a month that brought the chaos
bloodshed and tsunami of pain
a fallen angel was mistaken as an emotional drain
spirling down into the hell with the rain
a selfish animal with the vain
haunted stories, a beast no one has seen
a coward man
or baggage of expectation
a stone or invisible curtain
a shadow that protects but considered as disdain
a beast attacked the reigns
a trojan horse to breach the peace
a great fall into the depths of despair,
conceived a false narrative
a disaster planned as the natural one
terror in the moves
self-worth as down as the hope in pain
brutally violated the consent of innocence
tried to sell the soul

to achieve something that was gone
a faithful confession
at ease the army that had lost the battle
heavy arms and breath
Leonidas aiming at the Xerxes
a thousand arrow had gone through him
standing and roaring to fight back again,
a commitment to make the smile wake again
following the hardest terrain
a wish to meet in the end
a promise to wait eternally
an elliptical clock that teeth make
tree, sparrows, and squirrel were witnessing the change
a fall to catch the protagonist again
there has been constant fall since long ago
covering the wounds but making scars,
a saint had died long back ago
what about the youth that dies today?
do You care?
to hold the falling stars
I have seen dead bodies used as a boat to cross the river
don't blame me when I fall
as I haven't blamed that no one tried to catch
I was more than a drunk
who listen to the Opera and cry near the tomb
kiss me not when You can't see the pain caused by love
the sun has come nearby
the fog, that was made of distrust, has gone
I could see the sweat instead of rain
trust that will go on
nothing would quench the pain

lord had not been present at his houses
I have tried to set many appointments
return empty with exhausted hopes
I have seen the suffering created by him,
a month of return
time has come
go back to home
no one is insane
as the man who is in love;
see me not
'I am ashamed'
please hold me now as I beg
it would kill me, relieve me of this pain
a trauma that had happened in the past
an escape mechanism to survive the pain;
a hand that holds the man
a creature made out of compassion
a timeless love
nothing could break it, the iron curtain
that made me breathe again
I could dream again, to build a dream home
into far in the heart that has my name
with no reciprocity to sustain
a test that few will go through
a person who could love the beast in You
who could see the infant asking for acceptance
one who would be there even it meant to stand second
I see the faith restoring again
someone is there who would not bury me alive
who would wait till I breathe the last breath
to fall for me again

and to die with love
that both have in their chest, something sane
and something insane;

Kafkaesque

bourgeois earning bloodstain
white-collar oppressors
gaging the voices
coming out of the stomach
I see no virtue in sitting on a pile of grain
while the famine is causing starvation
Who made these rules?
who had signed the contracts?
the preconceived notion of people in power
moulding and bending rules to live
an illusion of growth, who holds the means
on the bottom down, a battle of survival
these corrupt termites eating the structure
a structure, that was promised to all
lies of equality and freedom
where are the culprits of human beings?
lords are decaying in their houses
materials produced out of blood and sweat
riding the human slaves
see, the lords of the modern world
with false hope of two-time meals
breaking the bones to clampdown them
fear in the eyes and hunger in the stomach
see the beautiful creatures of demigods
who was created to satisfy the lust
and needs of bourgeois
bureaucracy is a modern autocracy
endless forms to fill
and harsh punishment

when asked about filling the empty stomach
there are always two options
either to choose the side of powerful oppressors
or to stand for the weaker sect
repercussion become invalid
as one knows the brutality of lords
when challenged, the result is a massacre
man-made hunger and blame is on Gods
who is chained with golds and silver
lustrous materials blinded the lords
who couldn't see the people, standing in a queue;